To my parents

First published in Great Britain in 1995 by
Frances Lincoln Limited, 4 Torriano Mews
Torriano Avenue, London NW5 2RZ

Published in the United States of America by BridgeWater Books,
an imprint of Troll Associates, Inc.

Printed and bound in Hong Kong

10 9 8 7 6 5 4 3 2 1

Library of Congress Cataloging-in-Publication Data

Stow, Jenny.
Growing pains / Jenny Stow.
p.   cm
"First published in Great Britain in 1995 by Frances Lincoln Ltd.
... London" --T.p. verso.
Summary : Shukudu the young rhinoceros is afraid he will never grow
to have horns like his mother, even when he sees the other young
animals practicing the ways of their species.
ISBN 0-8167-3500-X
[1. Rhinoceroses --Fiction. 2. Animals--Fiction. 3. Growth-
-Fiction.] I. Title.
PZ7.S8895Gr   1995
[E]--dc20   94-35520

GROWING PAINS

JENNY STOW

BridgeWater Books

Deep in the African bush a rhinoceros was born. He was small and gray and always looked startled because everything was so strange and new.

His mother loved him dearly, and called him Shukudu.

When Shukudu was old enough, she took him down to the water hole. There he met the animals who came from far and wide across the hot, dusty land to drink.

Shukudu saw the young elephant and his mother with their long, curling trunks. He saw the young hippopotamus and his mother with their fat, rounded noses. He saw the tall giraffe and her mother bending their long, elegant necks to reach the water.

Shukudu's mother lowered her head to drink. Shukudu put his head down, too - and jumped back in surprise.

"Mother! What is that strange animal in the water?" he cried.

"That is your reflection, Shukudu. That is you," said his mother.

Shukudu took another look.

"But it can't be me. I'm a rhinoceros, and rhinoceroses have horns. That animal has no horns."

"Horns take time to grow," said his mother. "Be patient, Shukudu, and one day you will have horns just like mine." And as she smiled at him, her great horns looked more splendid than ever.

But Shukudu still didn't understand. "I look like nothing on Earth," he grumbled. "I will never look at my reflection again. Next time when I go to drink, I'll keep my eyes shut."

Poor Shukudu! He wanted so much to be a real rhinoceros. He watched his mother and tried to do everything just as she did. When other animals came too near she would snort loudly, lower her head to charge - and they would flee in terror.

But when Shukudu did the same thing to some gemsbok as they grazed, they just laughed and went on munching their grass.

The weeks passed, and Shukudu grew bigger.
He began to venture away from his mother
and explore the bush.

One morning, Shukudu saw a young stork
fluttering and zigzagging through the air.

"Hello, Stork. What are you doing?"
asked Shukudu.

"I'm learning to fly ... he-e-elp!" squawked
the stork, as she drifted slowly to the ground.

"Flying looks difficult," said Shukudu.
"But becoming a real rhinoceros is difficult, too."

"Just be patient," cried the little stork,
zigzagging off again.

Shukudu saw a bright yellow chameleon.

"Hello, Chameleon. What are you doing?" he asked.

"Practicing camouflage," the chameleon replied, changing quickly from yellow to orange, then to red. "But it's not easy."

"Camouflage looks tricky," said Shukudu. "But becoming a real rhinoceros is tricky, too."

"Just be patient," said the chameleon, always looking on the bright side.

Shukudu saw a young fruit bat in a tree.
    "Hello, Fruit Bat. What are you doing?"
he asked.
    "I'm learning to hang ...

... aaah!" The little bat's claws slipped from the branch and she fell to the ground. "Ouch! Learning to be a bat is tough."

"But becoming a real rhinoceros is tough, too," said Shukudu.

"Just hang on," said the fruit bat, climbing up again.

At dusk, Shukudu went back and told his mother about the stork, the chameleon, and the fruit bat.

"Mother, growing up is *so* difficult," he sighed, settling down beside her.

"Be patient, Shukudu," said his mother, and she gently nuzzled him until he fell asleep.

Months passed.

One bright, sunny day, Shukudu set off for the water hole.
He was looking forward to seeing his friends again.

At the water's edge he shut his eyes tightly,
lowered his head, and was just starting
to drink when he was startled by loud
screeches and squeals.

"Who's that?"

"It's Shukudu!"

"Just look at him!"
Shukudu perked up his ears.

"My, my!" squawked the stork, gliding
to the ground.

"Well done! You look magnificent," croaked
the chameleon, who was almost invisible
on a nearby branch.

"Yes, you do," squeaked a tiny voice
from a nearby tree. Shukudu looked up and
saw the fruit bat hanging from a branch.

"Just imagine," said the bat, "a real rhinoceros
at last!"

Shukudu was mystified. What did they all mean? There was only one way to find out.

He turned to the water and, instead of shutting his eyes, gazed into it. There, looking back at him, was a handsome rhinoceros - with two magnificent horns!

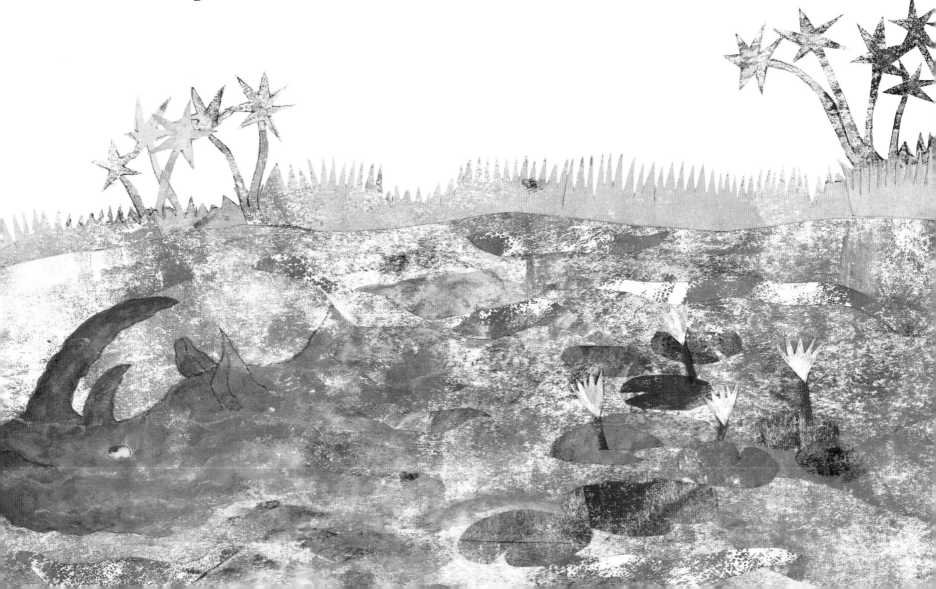

Shukudu couldn't believe his eyes. He gave a happy snort and galloped for joy. He lowered his head and charged the gemsbok, who fled in fright - until they realized it was their friend Shukudu. Then they were delighted, and complimented him on his splendid new horns.

And that night, when Shukudu fell asleep, he was the most contented rhinoceros in the African bush.